Scooter & Cupcake.

Written & Illustrated by
Mary Anne Lipousky-Butikas

ISBN-13: 978-1475209198
ISBN-10: 1475209193

Contact: mabutikas@yahoo.com

This book belongs to:

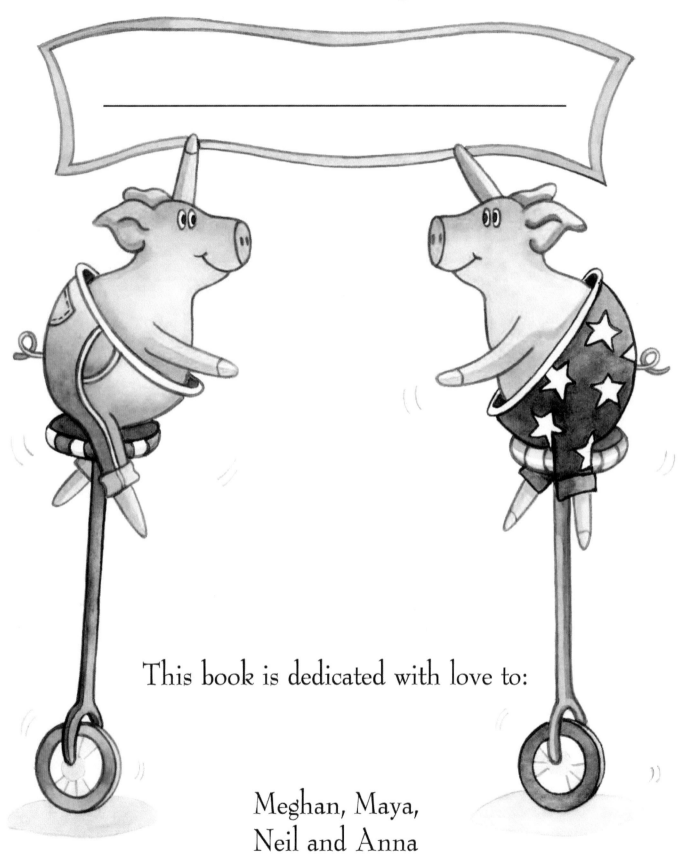

This book is dedicated with love to:

Meghan, Maya,
Neil and Anna

Scooter and Cupcake are a piggy pair,
best friends who always care.

They love to dance the piggy jig
and wear funny pants that are really big!

They're a team, a twosome
with caring hearts...

buddies, a duo and friends from the start.

Soft and pink
with piggy noses,
curly tails and
piggy poses.

They laugh and giggle,
oink and squeak...

and love the game
of hide-and-seek.

They share their things,
their thoughts and time...

chocolate chip cookies
and books that rhyme.

They share their Mommy and Daddy too...

Aunt Ida and Uncle Lou.

What's mine is yours and what's yours is mine,
and for two little piggies, that's just fine.

After all, a best friend is very good indeed
and just what two little piggies need.

They share their kites
and nighttime bears...

kettledrums and socks in pairs...

party cakes...

and lollipops...

beach toys...

and pillows that bop!

They share their swings and their pet fish.

They even share a birthday wish...

beach balls, skates...

and fruity treats...

jump ropes...

naps and breakfast wheats...

upside-down adventures...

and pretend
trips at sea...

little tin horns...

and cups of tea.

They share their cowboy hats and stars, cowboy boots...

and bugs in jars.

They share their colds and scary movies...

yoyos, sunglasses
and favorite woobies.

It couldn't have worked out any other way...

buds forever and here to stay

A twosome, a duo, a buddy, a mate...

for Cupcake and Scooter, the arrangement is great!

26488927R00028

Made in the USA
Charleston, SC
08 February 2014